Also by Jermesha Striblet-Holmes

Brown Girl Proverb: This Goes Out To All The Women And The Secrets They Keep
a Memoir.

Audrey ♥

love you
Babygirl!
you're so
supportive!

Jermesha Striblet-Holmes

LOSSES AND GAINS

Urban Fiction
A Chicago Narrative
Mathew 6:34
One days burden is enough for one day

Jermesha Striblet-Holmes

2019 Jermesha Striblet-Holmes

Jermesha Striblet-Holmes
LOSSES AND GAINS
All rights reserved. No part of this publication may be reproduced, stored in a retrieval system or transmitted in any form or by any means, electronic, mechanical, photocopying, recording, or otherwise without the prior permission of the author.

Published by:

Jermesha Striblet-Holmes
Chicago, IL 60644

ISBN-: 9781695869028
Imprint: Independently published

Table of Contents

GAINS

Introduction ……………………………….4

ONE……………………………………….8

TWO……………………………………..19

THREE…………………………………..29

FOUR……………………………………43

FIVE……………………………………..54

LOSSES

SIX……………………………………….62

SEVEN…………………………………..70

EIGHT…………………………………...78

NINE…………………………………….87

Letter From The Author……………….90

? ………………………………………...92

GAINS.

Introduction.

My name is Tiffany Shanté Gains, but most people know me as *"Tootie"*. My daddy gave me that nickname when I was younger and I'd only answer to it when he'd say it but, somehow it traveled out into the neighborhood. Some people don't even know my real name and honestly, I prefer it that way. So, Tootie it is. I'm from the west side of Chicago, a real city girl, but my mama moved us to the suburbs when I was fourteen. A lot of girls have it out for me but it's not like I don't know why. I'm pretty, I dress well, I'm not struggling and begging niggas for forty-dollars, and I haven't made any of these lame dudes my baby's father. Though that may not seem like a big deal, it's enough to make a female in my city *hate* you. But it's never been enough to make a female *touch* me. Partly because they could never get close to me and mostly because of who my mother is, Shawna Gains. I know her as *mama*, but the rest of the world knows her as "Lady Gains". She's known for her business and success, but she's noticed for her beauty. She's got a work ethic like Oprah, captivates and demands the room like Beyoncé and Michelle Obama. Tall, beautiful, chocolate skinned, curvaceous woman. Cheekbones that could reach the lips of God for just a peck. Thick and beautiful coily, brown hair that stretches across her head like the sun would the sky. That's Lady. That's my mama. But besides her euphoric looks, she's as gutter as they come. She grew up on Chicago Avenue and Lockwood with her three sisters: Trina, Lonnie & Shay, her twin. They were the original "city girls" of Chicago back in the 90s. They didn't mess with the jail birds and the drug dealers, they were only seen with rich ass business men. *"We wasn't no hoes. We was investments, and a man will only invest in something he truly cares about."* That's what my mama would always say.

  My daddy, Devon Gains, worked for himself as a financial advisor to some of Chicago's most elite businessmen and women. He met my mother at my uncle Kenny's birthday party, he's married to auntie Shay. Story is, my daddy was already familiar with who my mother was being as though his best friend was dating her twin sister. But, my mama never paid him any mind. That's how she is, only minding the business that pays her. That night, however, my daddy must've been paying her so much attention that she decided to give him some of her time. To make a long story short, three months later my daddy proposed and eleven months after that I came into the picture. During that time my daddy was still at the beginning of his career and my mama was his new partner. They tracked the ins and outs of every dollar each of their clients made, allowing them to better finance their own personal lives. Any idea my mama had my daddy invested in because she was right about it one hundred percent of the time. *"Bet on Lady Gains and you'll never lose."* That's her business slogan, she owns the Gains Finances franchise now since my daddy passed a few years ago in a car accident. But, since then Lady Gains has expanded the family business and began buying and flipping properties, making two or three times as much as they were worth. But that's not why her name holds so much weight, it's because of what she does outside of the business. She monitors the finances of some of Chicago's heaviest drug dealers, offering them advice in exchange for confidentiality and immunity, that way nothing looks suspicious on their ends and she gains some customer loyalty. There were a lot of families that lived comfortable lives because of my mama, so any female that wanted to come after me would be putting their uncle, father, brother or cousin in a real sticky situation. I guess that's why I don't have too many friends besides my cousin, Lump. He was auntie

Lonnie's oldest son, and her most complicated. Lump was the realest nigga I knew and the closest person to me besides my mama. With all the lame shit you see in the city, it's refreshing to know at least one thorough motherfucker out here. My father taught me a lot about men but Lump taught me a lot about niggas and if you don't already know the difference between the two you're about to find out. This past year I had to learn it the hard way.

ONE.

Today, I planned on relaxing. I had my line up of Netflix series I was going to watch and food already on the way. But, I don't know why I expected Lump *not* to find a way to get me up and moving. Which is why the moment his name flashed across the screen of my phone I knew everything I had planned would be put on pause.

"Aye, Tootie, what you on right now? I'm finna pull up."
"I'm at home, Lump."
"Aight, I got Twon with me. That's cool?"
I look at the phone and roll my eyes, "Why the hell you always got Twon with you, g? You know what's to him already."

Twon is Lumps bestfriend. He stays out south on 65th, he's tall and black as hell. He's good looking, though. He's about to start school at the University of

Michigan on a basketball scholarship this fall. He's been trying to talk to me for the last six months but I don't have the time nor energy to entertain a nigga right now. Especially, not one from out south. But, Lump seems to think we're the perfect match, which is why Twon is always with him anytime he comes to see me.

"Aye, he's not even on that. I promise. I'm pulling up now. Come out."

    I ran down all forty stairs in this big house mama moved us in a couple of years ago, it's only a few blocks outside of our old neighborhood. I swing the front door open and Lump is standing on the porch grinning like a kid on the playground. A lot of people think he and I are brother and sister because we're always with each other — you see me, you see Lump. On top of that we look just alike: round button noses, chocolate skin, big foreheads and big round hazel eyes. We were some pretty good looking kids thanks to our beauty queen mama's. He greets me with a shove to the head and a kiss on the forehead as usual. I look over and notice Twon leaning on Lumps car like it's his, attempting not to pay us any mind.

"Hey, Twon."
"Wassup, Tiffany."

He never calls me by my nickname and I never asked him why, I just assumed he was trying to be different. You know, calling himself trying to stand out from the rest of the dudes who wanted my attention.

"Y'all cute." I roll my eyes at Lump's comment and they land on Twon again who's *still* acting as if he's not paying us any attention. I can tell he just got a fresh line up from the white halo outlining his face. He looked good with his Nike tech and ones on, I knew he smelled good too because he always did. Of course, I'd never tell him that. He's got something good going for himself too, going to college and all. I have a year before I decide to head off to Howard, so maybe I'll let him come visit me then. My thoughts were halfway down the yellow brick road by the time I even noticed Lump calling my name.

"Tootie... TOOTIE!"
"Huh? Nigga, what is you yellin for?!"
"I *said* do you wanna slide to this kickback with us later tonight?"
"Who all gonna be there?"
"Here you go. It's just a small get together at JT's slot."
I shake my head, "That means Kiana and her ugly ass sister, Faye are gonna be there. You *know* they think I mess with JT."

"What does that mean? They ain't gonna do nothing and you know that. All they do is stare and wop… stare and wop… stare and wop."

We all start laughing as Lump attempts his best Faye and Kiana impression.

"Yea, Tiffany, just come. You already don't get out of the house," Twon adds.
"I do." I roll my eyes, "Aight, just come pick me up on y'all way there."
"Bet. Imma hit yo line later. Love you, babygirl.
"Love you too."

I watch Lump's car turn the corner and I stand on the porch for a minute before walking back into the house. But, before I could even touch the doorknob I hear someone yelling my name.

"*Tootieeeee! Tootie, baby! Hold on!*"

It's my grandmother, Mae Jenkins. Everybody calls her *Ma* because she's taken the whole damn neighborhood under her arms. She's the neighborhood cook, the babysitter, the mediator, everything. She has a heart of pure gold and the mouth of a sailor! She'd pray for you and curse you out all in the same breath. I'm sure that, that's why so many people loved her, she was real and she was approachable. The least judgmental person I knew. The most understanding person I knew. I love Ma.

"Hey, Ma! How you doin'? You walked all the way down here?
"Aw hell, child please. Them lil' three blocks ain't hurtin' nobody. Where ya mama at, baby? I gotta tell her something."
"She's upstairs, come on."

We walk into mama's room and she's in her purple and gold Kaftan and matching headscarf watching *House Hunters*. I jump on the edge of the bed and I'm instantly glued to Ma's wrinkled little mouth as she preps mama for whatever tea she has to spill. She's not that old, just past sixty, or at least that's what I assume. She never tells anyone her age and she honestly doesn't look a day over fifty. She's chocolate skinned, slim, and stands at five feet and five inches. My mama gets her height from Pop-Pop, may he rest in peace. But, Ma's beautiful just like mama and her sisters.

"Wassup, Ma? What you done heard now?", mama asks.
"Shawna, you won't believe what Shay done up and did this time."
"What, Ma?"
"That girl done took up all Kenny's money and ran off with it. She called me earlier crying, sayin' Kenny done cheated again."

Me and mama look at one another with half laughs. Auntie Shay has been running off on Uncle Kenny for years and doesn't do anything but run right back. The first time, he made a bad business deal and Auntie Shay wasn't too happy with it because it cost them a hell of a lot of money. So, she "ran off" with the rest of the money to "teach him a lesson" and came back three weeks later with an entirely new wardrobe explaining how she just needed time to breath. The second time she caught Uncle Kenny in bed with another woman and after trying to shoot both of their heads off, she emptied their joint account and fled to Jamaica. She was back home a week later because she said the heat gave her hives. So, this time we already knew the outcome.

"Ma, Shay *is* my twin but I swear we are nothing alike."
"I think it's 'cause I thought it was only one of you heffas in my womb and once the doctors told me it was two, all that wine I drank must've slipped right into her!"

We all start cracking up. I kissed her on the cheek and left the two of them in the room together to finish gossiping. I hope I don't have it as bad with men as Auntie Shay. That's why I don't bother with these niggas now.

    I hadn't realized how wrapped up in this new Netflix show I'd gotten and I completely forgot that I agreed to go to JT's kickback with Lump and Twon. I had about forty five minutes until I expected them to pull up so I took a quick shower, put some makeup on, got dressed, chose what wig I was feeling for the night and waited on his call. My phone rang and an unknown number swept across the screen. I answer and before I could say hello I hear Twon's voice on the other end telling me he and Lump are about to pull up. *Why in the hell is calling me?* and *why the hell did Lump give him my number?* The phone hangs up, I grab my purse, put on my shoes and head to the car. Once we pull up to his apartment I see two girls crossing in front of the car. It's Kiana and Faye switching their hips and adjusting their little ass shorts. Faye looks my direction and rolls her eyes so hard I could've sworn one rolled out of her head. She hates me over a nigga. The man buys me lunch *one* time and all of a sudden we're dating? I only asked him because he had a car and would always ride to McDonald's for lunch and bring it back to school. I got tired of eating that jailhouse lunch, so I asked him to get me a McChicken and fries — I even paid for it! But all Kiana and Faye saw was him bring the food to my table and walk off. You see, Faye and JT used to mess around, but Faye also isn't too soft on the eyes so I know I'm not his type at all. But, you know how girls are. Kiana spots me in the passenger seat and gives me a fake ass smile and wave. I remain still.

    We walked in to a cloud of smelly reggie smoke and a hint of whatever was in between these girls' legs. I was already ready to leave until I saw someone I recognized. It was my girl, Constance Valentine, everyone calls her Conny. She and I went to grammar school together before my mama moved us to the suburbs, but we still keep in touch. We were as thick as thieves growing up, from juke parties at the skating rinks to sleepovers on the weekends. She could out laugh, cry, dance and out drink anyone without a care in the world. That's what I loved most about her, what you saw was what you got. She didn't mess with too many people, especially not Kiana and Faye. But, seeing her out tonight wasn't out of the ordinary at all, she never missed a function.

"Wassup, Conny?!"
"Yaaasssss, Tootie is out of the house."
"Whatever. You know I don't do parties unless there's security and a bar. Basically anywhere this fake ID can get me in."

"Who'd you come with?"
"Lump."
"Aw okay."
"... and Twon."
"Aaaawwwww, okayyyyyyy." She says as she gives me a side eye.
"Chill out. He's just a plus one."
"Mhm."

    I grab whatever she's drinking out her hands and take a few sips. It's tequila, I hate tequila. I start to scan the room for anymore familiar faces and I come up short. I don't know why I always agree to go places like this with Lump, I rarely enjoy myself. About an hour goes by and I realize I haven't seen Lump nor Twon since we walked in, so I start patrolling the house looking for them. A "small get together" my ass, this place is packed with people. I make my way to the kitchen and I see Lump at the counter in some girls ear. I look to his left and I see Twon on his phone, I walk over and tap him lightly on the shoulder.

"Is this what you do at parties?"
He looks up from his screen and smiles. His teeth are perfect, like white glossy chiclets of gum.
"Yea, basically. You come checking up on niggas at parties?"
"Boy, bye. I was just looking for y'all, that's it."
"Or were you just looking for *me*?"

I look at him and roll my eyes.
"Y'all think y'all will be ready to go soon?", I ask while checking the time on my phone. It's already eleven and it looks like the party's just getting started.
"Damn, we just got here. I guess you ain't messin' with it, huh?"
"I'm about to get an Uber."
"Alone?"
"Yea, nigga."

    I walked over to Lump and interrupted his conversation and let him know I'm about to head out. He finally comes up for air after minutes of shoving his tongue down this girls throat and suggests Twon rides with me. Although it was what I wanted to do the least, I agreed to have Twon ride with me. It was pretty late and I wasn't as comfortable riding home alone as I'd seemed. I look at Twon and signal for him to come on. I hear Lump yell something as Twon and I leave the kitchen.

"Aw yea?!"
"I love you, Lump."
"I thought so. I love you too, babygirl."

    The Uber took three minutes to pull up and I got in the back hoping Twon would sit in the front, of course he didn't. I knew he'd try to spark up a conversation and I was not in the mood, so I put my headphones in and turned my music up as loud as it could go but that was no help. I felt him tap me on my leg but I acted as if I didn't even know he was touching me. We pulled up to my house and I damn near jumped out of the car and ran.

"Tiffany, hold up!"
"Yea?"
"What's the rush? Let me walk you to the door."
"We're at the door, Twon."
"You right... well let me talk to you before you go in."
"About what?"
"You know I'm leaving in a couple of months, we won't see each other for a while."
"Yea I know, I'm happy for you. Gettin' the hell outta Chicago."
"True. You gone miss me?"
"No."

He looked at me and shook his head while laughing.

"What's funny?"
"You wanna *not* like me so bad and it's just not working."
"How you figure that?"
"I can tell. But, you straight. I ain't gone do too much."

We stood in silence for a few seconds before saying bye and going our separate ways. This is why I should've taken the Uber alone.

TWO.

I wake up every morning to either the soultry sounds of Jill Scott or some new rapper that my mama has just discovered as her "new favorite." This week it's Gunna. The music usually sets the tone for the day and rap in the mornings means she's got some new money coming in.

"Mornin' mama. Wassup?"
"Tootieeeeeeee, Baby girl. I got some good shit comin' in today!"
"Above ground or underground?"

That's our code for whether this was legal or not. Above ground is regular Gains Financing, underground is that dirty money.

"Above."

"That's wassup. So, this means we've got a nice vacation coming up?"
"Hell yea. Dubai? Africa? Paris? Where to?"

    Me and mama have damn near traveled the world together. It used to be the three of us before daddy passed. I remember the year before he died we went to Tokyo for a week for his birthday, he loves Asian cuisine so it was perfect. We ate something new everyday and mama hated it! She vowed that we'd never go back there again just because she didn't enjoy the food. Daddy loved it, though.

"How about we go back to Tokyo?" I joked.
"Shoot, try again."
"Okay. How about Finland?"
"The happiest place in the world. Peaceful and thousands of miles away. Sounds like you're trying to get away from something, baby."
"Nah, it'd just be nice to be somewhere where we didn't have to worry about anything."
"Well, alright. Finland it is! Let's just hope they got some chicken spots to eat at."

***

    About a week and a half had gone by since Twon left me on my doorstep after that awkward conversation, so I hit up Lump to see what was up. I called him three times before he actually picked up the phone.

"Yo."
"Yo? Nigga. Why haven't I heard from you in almost two weeks?"
"My bad, baby girl. How you doin? How's teetee?"
"We good... You okay?"
"Yea I'm straight. Just picked up Lil Man for the week."

Lump has a two year old son with this disgusting excuse of a human being, Tasha. She hates Lump and she definitely hates me because Lump and I are so close, he tells me everything. So, I know about her trying to say that Lil Man wasn't Lump's son and how she tried to set him up just months after Lil Man was born. I want to fight that trick but Lump won't have it. He'd kill that girl if she ever touched me. Just as bad as Auntie Shay had it with men, Lump had it with women. I've never been a fan of the girls he dated or even slightly entertained, but he got a kick out of it. Girls loved him, they flocked like birds whenever he'd come around. Tasha was more like a mosquito, though, the only thing good about her was Lil Man.

I finally mustered up the courage to ask about Twon and Lump sure got a kick out of that as well. I'm sure he'll be letting him know I asked about him and end up making it a big deal. So I quickly changed the subject because I didn't need him milking this entire situation.

"You comin' to Ma's house Sunday? You know she ain't seen you in forever."
"Yea…"
I laughed. "Aight, nigga. I guess I'll see you *Monday*."

***

On Friday's I led cheerleading practice after school. I was co-captain this year so I wasn't playing any games with these new routines. The only downside to being on the team was sharing the spotlight with Kiana. She only had a sudden interest to be on the team once Faye convinced the whole Junior and Senior classes that JT and I were talking. Any opportunity she got to get close to me she took it. Funny thing is, she and I were really close friends our Freshman year. Our lockers were right next to one another and we had the same homeroom and lunch period, so we had plenty of time to grow closer. It wasn't until Faye started high school that everything spiraled out of control. Kiana was extremely protective over Faye due to the fact that she'd spent most of her time in grammar school being bullied for how she looked, and it only got worse once she got to Mel High.

The day Faye got her ass beat in the cafeteria bathroom was the day Kiana and I's friendship ended. She thinks I set Faye up because I knew the girls who had jumped her. Ever since then she's hated me and this JT mess hasn't made it any better.

"ALRIGHT LADIES I NEED TO SEE '*Mel High Fly*' FULL OUT!" I yelled.
"Mel High Fly? We've only done that routine twice, I don't remember that shit." Kiana whined.
"Kiana, just do what you can and I'll correct whatever mistakes you make after."
"Girl, you are *co*-captain. Calm down."
"And you are *un*prepared. Sit this one out."

    She stomped all the way out of the gymnasium and received none of the attention she was craving. Yea, I may be co-captain now, but just wait until next year. Until then, however, I'll stand in my power as co-captain. "*Stand in your power, Tootie.*" That's what my daddy would tell me while growing up. I had terrible anxiety and low self-esteem which caused me to remain quiet and shrink in rooms full of people even when it was necessary that I stood out. I joined the cheerleading team seven months before my daddy passed and it's been one of the best decisions I've made throughout my high school career— minus letting Kiana join the team. I remember one game she attempted to call out a cheer as if me and Jada, the captain, were all of a sudden invisible. But, the squad follows *our* command, not hers, so she just stood there looking stupid. This is why I want to go to Finland, to get away from people like her; the ignorant kind.

After practice I took an Uber to Uncle Remus and ordered my usual: two piece, fried hard, with extra mild sauce on the fries. I took my next Uber over to Conny's place, showing up unannounced was never a problem. I knocked on the door and saw her younger brother peeking through the blinds. The next person I saw was her older sister, Angel, opening the door.

"Wassup, Tootie. Conny's upstairs in her room."

I walk up to her room and see her on the floor with her legs crossed and eyes closed meditating. She was a psychedelic, earthy ass chick. Incense burning, lit candles that smelled of vanilla, sage all around, weirdly shaped stones in all sorts of colors. Shit was cool as hell to me, but a lot of people thought it was weird for a black girl to be into all of this stuff. But, I didn't care so I just let her finish "aligning her chakras" as she would put it.

"Wassup, love? What brings you to my humble abode?"

"Shit. I didn't feel like going home. You got any plans for tonight?"
"Just Netflix."
"Welp. Get the snacks ready, I'll find us a show to binge watch."

We were about two episodes in to *Jane The Virgin* when I got a text from an unknown number. It was Twon.

```
Hey, Tiffany. It's Twon. Wyo?
```

```
                    Netflix at Conny's. Wbu?
```

```
At the gym with the guys.
Thought I'd see how you were doin…
since you asking about me and all
```

I shook my head and thought, "Bug ass, Lump."

```
   I was just making sure you were good.
```

```
For someone who doesn't like me,
it def sound like you care
```

```
                              Whatever.
```

```
Let me see you tonight. I'll come to
Conny's before I head over to Rell place
```

> ```
>                    You can't just
>           pop up at people's houses.
> ```

```
I'm not, I'm poppin up
at Conny's house, lol
```

    I checked with Conny to make sure it was cool and she said she was fine with it. Her parents weren't strict at all so the extra company didn't bother them either. There was a knock on the door about thirty minutes later. Twon stood there in his basketball shorts, a white t-shirt and some 11's. He hugged me and walked right in like he owned the place. For someone who had just come from the gym, he smelled good as hell. We walked over to the couch and sat down. It was quiet for about a minute before I broke the silence.

"So, wassup?"
"Tiffany, when you gone stop playin'?
"What are you talkin' about?"
"I been tryna get with you for months now. I respect yo' space. I gave you yo' time. I'm a gentleman. Yet, you still act like you don't want nothin' to do with me."

    He's right. I don't have anything bad to say about Twon, I'm just not interested in being with anybody right now. Even though he seems like a great dude, I don't want those problems — relationship problems.

"I'm not trying to be in a nigga face at the moment, Twon. It's nothin' personal."
"So what *are* you trying to do? Cause whatever it is I'll do it with you."
"I'm just chillin'."
"Well, I guess we just chillin' then. What y'all watching up there?"

We make our way up to Conny's room and she's had the show paused the entire time I was downstairs. I took my spot on the beaned bag and he plopped down on the floor next to my legs. Three episodes later, Conny was knocked out and Twon suggested he head over to Rell's before it got too late. We walked back downstairs and I opened the door and before I knew it Twon's lips were laying on mine. Who the hell told him to do *that*? Honestly, who the hell cares? I liked it.

"It was nice chillin' with you, Tiffany. I'll get up with you soon."
"Okay. Cool"

He was in his car and half way down the block before I had time to register what had happened. Did I just let this nigga kiss me? I *knew* I should've taken that Uber alone that night.

THREE.

Sometimes you have to encourage yourself
The pressure is all around but God is present help
The enemy created walls but remember giants, they do
fall
Speak over yourself, encourage yourself in the Lord

    I walk into Ma's house and hear her favorite church song playing, faintly, in the background. The smell of fried chicken snuck it's way up my nose and led me right to the cook, herself. Ma could cook anything and it tasted like heaven on earth. Sunday's were my favorite because I'd have enough to-go plates to last me the next three days. Sunday's were also family day, it reminded me a lot of *Soul Food*.

"Ma, did you make the cake?", I asked.
"That's all this child care about is this damn lemon pound cake. You don't see all this good cooking goin' on girl?"

She points to the cake sitting on the other side of the counter, it's still warm so I cut me a piece. There's nothing like Ma's lemon pound cake.

"Is Lump coming by today? I know y'all joined at the hip."
"He said he would, Ma."
"Mhm. If I didn't have you you'd swear I didn't have any grandchildren at all…a damn shame."
"Aw, Ma. It's not even like that. I'm the baby of the bunch so I have a lot more time on my hands to be with you, that's all."
"Mhm. Where's ya mama?"
"She had to drop some things off at the office, she'll be here soon."

"Familyyyyy. What's goood? What's hap'nen!?"

A tall, light skinned man wearing cargo shorts, a plain white t-shirt and Birkenstocks, comes barging into the kitchen with open arms. It's Lumps daddy, Uncle Will. Remember how I mentioned my mama and her sisters only dated the rich and fine men back in the day? Well, a little bit before that my Auntie Lonnie met Uncle Will at a steppers set. They fell in love hard and fast, which explains Lump being conceived after only a few weeks of them knowing one another. Unfortunately, he and Auntie Lonnie split when Lump was about a year old. He wasn't rich and fine then and he's even further from it today, but he's family; always smiling and always around.

"Will, why won't you shut the hell up with all that yellin' and carryin' on? But, hey baby, how ya doin'?"
"I'm blessed, Ma. I'm blessed."
"Hey, Uncle Will."
"Tootie Frootie! How's my favorite niece?"
"I'm good, Unc."
"How's, uh… how's Junior?

Lump and Uncle Will don't really have a relationship. Mostly because Uncle Will hasn't necessarily been father of the year. He rarely visited Lump after he and Auntie Lonnie split and he kept it that way. He'd send birthday cards and a few dollars here and there but that was about it.

"He's good. As always." I answered.
"Well that's lovely… that's just lovely."

The next face I see peeking around the corner is Auntie Trina's. She must've snuck through the back to surprise Ma, it's been so long since she'd seen her. Auntie Trina moved to Atlanta after college to pursue her managing career, but she comes home for holidays and special occasions and every once in awhile she'll surprise Ma on Sunday's.

"*Heyyyy foxy lady.*" She sang as she wrapped her arms around Ma from behind, swaying back and forth, "*How you doin sista girl?*" Ma turns around and grabs Auntie Trina's face as tight as she can and lands a big old kiss right in the middle of her forehead. If you've never seen a more affectionate family, you have now. She looks over at me and crouches down in a twerking position and starts shaking her big butt all over me. This is how she's always greeted me. She's Ma's youngest child and it shows.

"Where's Lady?", Auntie Trina asked.
"She's at the office, she's on her way."
"I see Will's ugly self so I'm guessing Lonnie ain't here yet. I know I won't be seeing Shay either since she's on the run again. So, I guess I'll be making the banana pudding."
"How's Atlanta?", I ask.
"Messy. Gay. Hot. Busy. I love it! I just started representing this new singer and she's *cold*."
"That's wassup, maybe I can come down and visit later this summer." She looked at me with hesitation to answer. Auntie Trina doesn't like people in her space which is *also* why she moved all the way to Atlanta.
"I'd love to have you as a house guest, niece. Just you, right?"
"Yea. I think Lump can survive a few days without me."
"Doesn't he cramp your style? How you gone get you a nigga and he's always glued to your hip?"

"I don't want a nigga, Auntie."

I was becoming irritated by the direction the conversation was going and felt relief once I heard the clicking of my mamas heels coming from the front door.

"Hey, Trin. Hey, Ma."
"*Lady Gains*. How have you been?"
"I'm good, I'm good."

Mama and Auntie Trina were very short with each other for good reasons. About three years ago they fought right here in this same spot because Auntie Trina was an hour late to dinner. She stopped off to see some man and didn't think to tell anyone she was going to be late. When she finally walked through the door all hell broke loose and once my mama gets going there's no slowing down. Before we knew it mama had shoved Auntie Trina in her head and shit went down. They have the shortest tempers out of the family and the smartest mouths to match so the less they said, the better. Thank God, the food was ready so we could avoid any future ass whoopings.

***

Since Lump hadn't shown his face yesterday for Sunday dinner I knew I could expect to see him today after school. We only had about a month left before school let out for the summer so he'd pick me up a few days out of the week to avoid me getting caught up in anything crazy. Chicago niggas in the summertime are a different breed and I'm not trying to be an undeserving target. The murder rate seems to be increasing every year, it's ridiculous. That's why Lump insists on picking me up as often as he can because he's seen first hand what the street shenanigans are all about. He used to be heavily involved with the gang life up until he had Lil Man, and because of what I saw him experience I used to fear him being the next name running across the screen on WGN. As smart as he is, involving himself in that lifestyle was the dumbest thing he had ever done. Lil man saved him.

As soon as I see Lump getting ready to turn the corner I say goodbye to the squad and I meet him at the curb. I get in and I can barely make out his face! He was three different shades of black and blue. His left eye was shut closed and he had bloody cotton balls in both of his nostrils. He was so beat up he could barely speak, let alone move. It's a miracle he made it this far from wherever this shit happened.

"Lump, what the fuck?!", I yelled as I started searching for shit in my bag as if I was the type to carry around a first aid kit and whatever-the-hell else this nigga need to sew his damn face back together.
"Imma pull over on the next block and get in the passenger seat. I need you to drive, okay?"
"Nigga, what the hell happened to your face?"
"Get me to the house first, Tootie."

    I hop into the driver's seat and speed all the way home, I know I messed his car up with all the potholes I neglected to dodge. I didn't care, I just needed some answers. I had to carry him all the way up the stairs to the guest bathroom. By this time he's damn near delusional; words slurring, mumbling all types of *bitches* and *muthafuckas* under his breath. How did this nigga manage to drive to school to even pick me up?

"Lump, get it together. What happened?"
"Tay and his niggas jumped me. I'm coming out the liquor store and they instantly, run up on me. Only reason I know who it was is 'cause I saw the car pull off."
"Why would Tay target you, though? Ain't yall cool?"
"Nah, we just cordial. I don't do no politickin'."
"So... what you gone do?"
He looked me dead in the eyes and said, "Handle it."

I stood there looking at him hunched over the toilet. I'd never seen Lump this beat up and it scared the hell out of me.

***

I couldn't get the image of Lump all beat up out of my head. He hadn't "handled" anything yet but I was still on edge. I didn't want him to do anything that would land him in jail, leave Lil Man without his daddy or me without my best friend. I needed to relieve some stress so I called Twon. I'm sure he was already caught up on what was going on so he would understand what I was feeling. I scrolled through my messages and found our conversation thread. Is it bad that I still hadn't saved his number even after he kissed me? The call went straight to voicemail but I wasn't calling his ass again —I wasn't desperate. Besides, I didn't have to because a few minutes later his number popped up on my screen and I answered.

"Wassup, Twon."
"Tiffany. How you doin lil baby?"
"Honestly, I'm off my square after all this stuff with Lump. Ain't that mess crazy?"
"Yea…"

The tone of his voice had me a bit uneasy. Why didn't he seem to be as concerned as I was? I mean, grant it, Lump is *my* cousin but he and Twon are like bestfriends. Maybe, he's just in shock.

"You got any insight on what Lump might have up his sleeve?"
"That's nothing you need to be worrying about. Let the men handle that. You just worry about the next time we gone see each other."
"Come by tonight, I need the company."

    It was about an hour and a half before Twon showed up at my doorstep. This would be the first time he actually came inside my house so it was a bit awkward. My mama didn't play that "having boys in your bedroom" shit, so we chilled in the TV room. With the movie theatre set-up it was less of a chance he'd try anything that'd have us horizontal instead of vertical, if you know what I mean. He looks really good, better to me than usual. I guess that's what happens once you start liking someone, you start paying attention to things you hadn't noticed before. For instance, he had a few beauty marks under each of his eyes. His brows were really thick and always looked arched and clean. He had a smile like Bill Bellamy and LL Cool J, every time he'd show them pretty white teeth I felt my knees giving out.

"What you staring at?" he asked while grabbing my leg to rest on top of his.
"Boy, ain't nobody starin' at you."
"Alright, Tiffany. So what we watchin' tonight?"
"Umm... Brown Sugar?"
"What you know about Brown Sugar?"
"Please.", I say while rolling my eyes. "I've watched it *atleast* a hundred times."
"So, you like black love stories and shit like that?"

He started looking at me like I had shape shifted into Sanaa Lathan or something. I can tell where this conversation was going so I played along, I wasn't holding back this time.

"Yea, I do."
"You think you could see yourself loving me one day?"
"I mean... if you give me something worth loving, yea."
"Something like what?"
"I've only ever seen something similar to what I've wanted on TV screens and from my daddy. From what I can tell, a good man supports his woman. He loves her and all of her shit because he knows she's worth everything, even the bullshit. He respects her for being who she is and not just who he wants her to be. That's how my daddy seemed to treat my mama. I don't think he ever cheated because he had everything he wanted and he knew that... something like that."

"Damn."
"Yea, that's the reaction I get from most niggas."
"Chill out. I'm only sayin' that 'cause most girls I've dealt with have never given me an answer like that. They usually say something bout 'havin a bag' and someone 'taking care of them.' Any nigga can give you forty dollars and some time, but you clearly want more."

At this point he's about three inches from my face, hand on my upper thigh and I'm pretty sure this nigga is trying to open the vortex to my soul by the way he's staring into my eyes. He's gonna kiss me again and we haven't even started the movie. I was only expecting this to happen once his ass was halfway out the door!

"You wanna… you wanna start the movie now?" I said while using my only free hand to search for the remote while my eyes were still glued to his.
"Nah, not really."
"You want a snack or somethin'."
"Uhn-Uhn."
"Well what you want, nigga?"
"You."

Shit. What I wasn't about to do was give this nigga some while we were just a few feet from my mama's bedroom. I wasn't planning on doing any of this anytime soon, period. I had to stop him and I had to do it *quick,* so I hop up from my chair and tell him I have to go to the bathroom.

"I gotta pee. I'll be right back."
He laughs a little and says, "okay."

    I get to the bathroom and immediately text Conny.

```
Biiiiitttcchhhh.
```

                                            What's tea?

```
Twon's here.
```

                        Oh. So y'all *freakin*?

```
Girl, we ain't doin nothin.
I just acted as if I had to
pee and now my dumb ass
stuck inna bathroom.
```

                Girl, just tell him it's that
          time of the month. If he ain't nasty
                        he'll fall back, lol.

```
Oh, so this is funny to you?
You know what, I got this. Bye
```

I run the faucet for a couple of seconds and flush some imaginary pee down the toilet. I start walking back to the room and, to my surprise, this nigga ain't there. I can't call out because my mama is asleep, so I started searching for this man *in my own house*. I go downstairs to check and see if his shoes are still at the front door. They're there, just how he left them. I start walking towards the kitchen and he isn't there either, doesn't this nigga know it's rude to just wander throughout people's homes without permission? I notice the downstairs bathroom door is closed and I'm instantly relieved to know that, unlike me, this nigga really had to pee. I start to knock until I hear him talking on the phone.

"Yea, she upstairs. She prolly wondering where I went, so wassup?"

Is this nigga talking to another girl moments after trying to freak on me? I knew I should've taken that Uber by myself that night! If it's one thing a nigga's got, it's *the audacity*.

"I'm not about to just up and leave this girl house out of nowhere. Just meet me in about an hour or so."

I'm standing there thinking, "*wowwww, this shit is beyond me.*" He's about to *see* her too?! I got so irritated to the point where I started banging on the door. He pops his head out with this puzzled look on his face.

"You good?"
"Am *I* good? Who you about to meet in 'a hour or so'?"
"You tweakin'. That's business, not no bitch. Let's go back upstairs."

I look at him with my sharpest, most cut throat stare while trying to read in between the lines. Either he was a really good liar or he was actually telling the truth, either way I was convinced and now I feel like a goofy.

"My bad. If you gotta go you can just go now."
"Girl, come here."

He kisses me long and hard, at that moment I didn't want him to leave at all. This was all bad. I had caught feelings after trying to discipline my emotions and I could already see this becoming a problem. Niggas have never benefited me in any way, nothing even as small as a conversation. Yet, here I am letting this boy kiss all of the common sense out of my body.

Damn.

FOUR.

It's been about three weeks since I've heard anything from Lump and it has my anxiety going haywire. I know he and Twon don't want me involved in anything, but damn, it's not like I want to hold the gun up to whoever's head. I just want to know what's up so that I can be prepared to help put out the fire. If not me, then we all know who can clean this shit up if need be. Aside from my newfound love interest and Lumps situation, I have other things going on. Something that has absolutely nothing to do with any of this. I called Conny up and asked her to meet me at the mall so I could run something by her. These were the moments I was thankful to have someone other than Lump as someone I could trust with information. She doesn't know as much as Lump but she has definitely been helpful with a lot thus far. It's not too common that you find a female friend whom you can trust and have trusted for so long. Conny's, that girl. Conny's, that one.

I was expecting her to have made it to the mall by now. I had been here for about thirty minutes, eyeing the clothing racks in Zara. She said she would be running behind but I was entirely too anxious to have any patience. Another twenty minutes had passed before I finally spotted her walking out of Borders. I know damn well this girl wasn't reading books this entire time.

"Hey, girl. Sorry, I'm late."
"You good. Let's go up to Potbelly's or something and talk there. All that waiting has me hungry."

We make our way up the escalator and find a cozy corner to sit inside the restaurant. As hungry as I was, I couldn't push myself to eat anything.

"Alright, so wassup?"
"I got something to tell you…"
"Bitch… you pregnant? I thought you and Twon wasn't touchin'! But, wait. How'd it happen that fast? Ain't it kinda early?"
"Girl, shut up! I'm not pregnant."
"Well, what is goin' on?"
"You remember when I disappeared for that weekend a few months ago? Well, I went somewhere to find something… or should I say someone."
"Okay, Inspector Gadget, who'd you find?"

"My sister."
"Since when do you have a sister, Tiffany?"
"Since August of 1996. She's only a few years older than me. Her name is Jream — Jream Sinclair Jenkins."
"Well, why doesn't she have the same last name as you if she's your sister?"
"She was adopted and all that shit changed. She was in New Orleans the entire time, but I found her and I'm gonna find a way to get her to come here and visit for a while."
"So, do yo mama know anything about all this? Does she know that the daughter she put up for adoption is comin to visit for a family reunion?" she asked sarcastically.
"Nah, she doesn't know. But, I'm gonna tell her today."
"Whew, child. Well, where do I come in at? I know you not just telling me all of this for nothin'."
"I need you to keep her for me tonight."
" Ton— you tellin' me this girl is *here* already? Where's she at, Tamera? Where's Tia?"
"This isn't funny, Conny! She's here in the mall, I'm about to text her now."

    I couldn't believe I'd seen this adventure the entire way through. I have a sister, a beautiful sister. She looks just like me and my mama and I know you're wondering how all of this even happened so, here's the backstory:

    Before my mama met my daddy, she was kicking it with this dude everyone called Ghost. He was nothing like my daddy; he was rough and rugged and spent most of his time in the streets and on my grandmama's couch. To make a long story short, he got my mama pregnant. The only issue was he was prepared to play daddy but my mama wasn't at all on board. Abortion was never apart of her plan so adoption was her only option. I can only imagine how Ma felt watching her baby carry her own child, but she stuck by her side. Once mama had Jream she handed her off to her new family immediately after the birth, leaving no room for attachment. She never spoke of anything after that day, at least not until a few months ago. It was Sunday at Ma's place and everyone was there. Like any other family function, the food ran low and the drinks started pouring. I guess Uncle Will had one too many and started acting his shoe size, causing a huge argument between him and Auntie Lonnie. She started sending shots his way and he started sending them everywhere else! In the midst of his outburst, Auntie Lonnie yelled out how she should've listened to her sisters and never dealt with him to begin with. That's how I found out there was a missing puzzle piece.

"SHOULD'VE NEVER DEALT WITH ME?! AT LEAST I STUCK AROUND LONG ENOUGH TO KNOW WHO MY DAMN CHILD WAS! AIN'T THAT RIGHT, LADY? Y'all ain't nothin but a bunch of fake ass hoes. A bunch of Build-A-Bitches."

The moment he spat those allegations at my mama her entire face fell to the floor. I'd seen my mother's face tell many things, but shame was never one of them. Of course she blamed it on Uncle Will's drinking but I wasn't folding. I started researching everyday, looking through old pictures and trying to piece together something I knew nothing about. I finally came across a picture of my mama and some light skinned man with his arm wrapped around her neck. This was the only picture of them two so I knew it must've either meant something, or nothing at all.

The words "Ghost and Lady 4L" were written on the back in my mama's handwriting. I took the picture and showed it to Lump, hoping he knew something that I didn't.

"My mama has a picture with this nigga in it, too. I think he was my daddy's best friend's brother or some shit like that… Justice. Yea, that's his name."

If you knew me, all I needed was a name and I could find anyone on the internet. I already knew where he was from and who he knew, so I got down to business. Turns out the nigga stayed out south with an entire family. I wasn't dumb enough to go knocking on the man's door asking to see my sister, so instead I just sent him a friend request on Facebook. A few days later he inboxed me:

```
You look just like your mama and your
sister. It must've taken you a good
amount of snooping to come across my
page. So what do you wanna know. Ask me
anything.
```

    All of a sudden I forgot everything I wanted to know. So, I started with the obvious question:

```
                    Where's my sister?
```

```
She's not with me if that's what you're
thinking. But, I keep up with her from
time to time. She's in New Orleans,
finishing up her undergrad at Xavier
University. I have all her information
if you want it.

Jream Sinclair Jenkins
1 Drexel Drive
New Orleans, LA
St Martin Deporres Hall
```

I thanked him and immediately made plans to visit her. I told my mama it was another college interest I had and she bought my ticket and booked my room for the weekend. Everything seemed to be working out just fine until I realized I hadn't planned what I was going to tell this girl once she saw me. What if she doesn't respond how I expect her to? If she's anything like our mother she's going to be hard to convince. Aside from the angst, I was extremely excited to be meeting my sister for the first time. Lump was like my brother but having a sibling of my own felt great, especially because she was a girl. That's like having a built in best friend. Once the plane landed I caught an Uber to my hotel and dropped all of my things off there. I wasn't the least bit tired with all of this adrenaline rushing through my veins. I immediately called another Uber to the university and found my way to the admissions office. I told them I was looking for my sister, I gave them the address and they showed me exactly where to go. It was still pretty early in the day and I didn't have her schedule or anything so I just waited inside of her dorm like a weirdo until I saw her. Ghost sent me a picture of her yesterday and I haven't been able to take my eyes off of it so I knew exactly who I was looking for. She was tall and a bit lighter than me. She had a round button nose and slanted eyes just like I did, only they were grey. She had a head full of kinky, curly hair that she'd dyed a sandy brown color. She was beautiful and looked just like Lady with just a hint of her father.

I waited for at least an hour before I saw her walking through the doors of the building. I got up and rushed to the elevator before she got on and I stood there next to her as stiff as a beauty supply store weave and avoided all eye contact. She ended up breaking the silence:

"Wassup, luh girl."
"Lil girl?"
She starts laughing, "Oh you not from here, huh?"
"No, I'm not. But, hey."
"Where ya from?"
"Chicago. The city."
"Fuhreal? One of my luh juvies from out there. You look kinda young, you here for a college visit?"
"Um, yea, something like that. I have some family out here, too."
"Aw yea? What's their names I might know em?"

I paused for a couple of seconds and then I just blurted it out. What the hell else was I going to do? I had all of two days left here and I wasn't going to waste them pretending.

"My sisters name is Jream."
She looked at me, "My names Jream, and I only know one Jream and that's me." I just stood there like a fool without saying anything.
"What's her last name?"
"Jenkins. Jream Sinclair Jenkins."

    Once the elevator stopped she grabbed my hand and whisked me down the hall. We walked about four doors down until we got to what I assumed to be her room. There was pink shit everywhere, along with a boatload of pictures and posted notes on every corner of the walls. We may be sisters but we definitely don't have the same taste in anything.

"Alright, so you tellin' me we family? How? All my family is here, luv."
"I don't wanna have to be the one to break it to you but, if you don't already know, y—…"
"I'm adopted. Yea, I know."
"How much do you know about us, then?"

    She paused and looked at me real hard. It's crazy how much she resembled our mother, her nose flared up just like hers whenever she was analyzing anything. Her body language matched hers to a T! It was all there, the hair, the cheekbones, the *everything*! It was undeniable.

"You look like me."

"And you look just like our mama, just a bit lighter. My name is Tiffany, Tiffany Gains." I reached my hand out to shake hers.

"So, you came all the way to Louisiana to give me a handshake?"

She's right, I hadn't thought any of this shit through and I can tell she was already growing irritable.

"I came here to get to know you and to possibly convince you to come to Chicago at some point or another. My mama — *our* mom would be well up to date by then, so you wouldn't have anything to worry about."

"Girl, I got buku shit that I handle out here, I can't just come to yo city. Plus, I don't even know you."

"Look, I'm here for another day and a half. We can get to know one another and before I leave you can make your own decisions about visiting. I just found out I had a sister a few weeks ago and I'm looking at her for the first time ever. This shit is overwhelming as hell for me just as it is for you, but I'm here! Let's just make the best of it."

She sat in silence for about thirty seconds before saying anything. I was sure she was going to kick my black butt out, but instead she just looked at me and asked, "*You want a cold drink?*" We sat and talked for hours after that and it turned out we had way more in common than I expected. She hated the smell of cinnamon, she loves doing her makeup and hair, her favorite food is steak and she sings! I was like a kid in a candy store, glued to her every word. I couldn't wait to get her back home so the rest of the family could meet her.

***

    I texted Jream to meet Conny and I at Potbelly's, she said she was just finishing up at the register in Victoria's Secret and would be on her way up. Finally, she came strutting into the restaurant with bags in each of her hands. She took the seat next to me and introduced herself to Conny. All of us laughed after I gave a rundown of how Jream and I met. I finally felt lighter after introducing my sister-friend to my *actual* sister. Now, the only thing to do from here was to tell Lady what I had gone and done.

FIVE.

I woke up to RodyRich's *"Every Season"* playing this morning so I knew it was the best time to break the news to my mama about Jream. She spent the last few nights at Conny's waiting for my cue to come on over. Today had to be the day or I'm almost positive Jream will be on the next flight back to NOLA.

"Goodmorning, mama."
"*Great*morning, TootieBootie. How'd you sleep?"
"I slept okay…"

I guess she caught on to the fact that I was avoiding all eye contact because she stopped plating my breakfast and walked around the counter to stand directly in front of me.

"Why you ain't lookin' at me?"
"Cause.."
"Cause, *what?*"

"Cause, I got something to tell you and I don't know how you're gonna react."

"Aw *shit*. Yo ass is gotdamn pregnant. Tootie, I *told* you to keep yourself protected." She started pacing the kitchen like a hype off of Madison and Pulaski, I had to snap her out of it.

"Ma, I ain't pregnant. Chill out."

"Is everything okay with Lump?"

"Yea, it's not Lump."

"Well, what the hell is it, Tiffany?"

"I … um … I met someone. Her name is Jream."

"Soooo… you like girls? Tiffany, that's not a problem in my heart. Love who you wanna love."

"Lord, Jesus mama. Jream is not my lover, she's my sister."

She stopped stirring the grits and I got ready to duck because they could come flying my way at any second. Her hands dropped to her side and she stood there in silence for what felt like an eternity. Finally, she turned around and looked me dead in the eye and asked, "Ok, well where is she?" "She's at Conny's. She's been there for the last two days waiting for me to let her know when it was okay for her to finally come over. She's really cool, ma." She shook her head and wiped her hands on her apron. I can tell she had a lot of questions but she didn't ask any of them. Instead, she walked over to where I was sitting and hugged me:

"I'm glad. It's about time my girl came home."

After that she walked off to her bedroom and left me sitting at the kitchen counter, just as tense as I had been in the beginning. I immediately texted my address to Jream. It was time for her to meet her mama.

***

Conny dropped Jream off that night around nine. My mama was sitting in the living room with her favorite glass of red wine awaiting her estranged daughters arrival. She walked in and took a seat adjacent from me and directly across from my mother. For a minute they just stared at one another without saying so much as "hello." I damn sure wasn't about to contribute to the conversation being as though I had done enough as it is, so I just sat there with them. I wondered what was going through my mother's head: Was she secretly cursing me out? Was she practicing what'd she say to the daughter she put up for adoption twenty-two years ago? I couldn't take the silence for much longer.

"Mama, this is Jream. Jream, mama."
"Yea, I figure that much, luv." Jream said.
"It's nice to see you all grown up. I'm sure you probably have a lot of questions for me, so go ahead."

"No, not really. I kept in contact with my birth father and he pretty much told me everything."
"What'd Ghost tell you?"
"Basically, you weren't ready for a baby and he was. I don't fault you for that though, ya heard me. I'm older than you were when you had me and I know damn well I don't want no lil one right now."
"I guess he got it right this time. How'd you run into Tiffany?"
"It was more like her running into me down in New Orleans. She reminds me a lot of myself."
"Yea, once she gets going she doesn't really take 'no' for an answer. Well, you're here now and more than welcome to stick around for however long you want. Besides, we've got a lot of catching up to do."

    Jream had been with us for two days and my mama was already adjusting to having both of her girls around 24/7. They were instantly in sync with one another, it was like they'd been together each others whole lives. All I kept thinking about was how my daddy would've received his new stepdaughter. He loved me like I was his most prized possession and I'm sure he would've done the same with Jream. We had been cooped up in the house for so long that I forgot all about introducing her to Lump. I ran down an entire list of people that Jream has to meet, with Lump and Ma being at the very top. Mama looked at me as if to say I was going too far, but how'd she expect to hide the fact that she'd reunited with her long lost daughter from the rest of the family? At that moment I also realized Jreams family back in New Orleans had absolutely no idea what was taking place here either.

"Tootie, I think that we should wait a little while before we share this with everyone. You can tell Lump but don't take it any further just yet."
"Alright. We can go meet up with him now. C'mon Jream."

   I ordered an Uber and about fifteen minutes later we were on our way over to Lumps apartment. I didn't bother calling to let him know that I was on the way because I made it a habit of showing up to his place unannounced. Luckily for me I never came by while he was entertaining some girl, so hopefully this is another one of those times. Once we pulled up to Lumps building I immediately recognized the car parked in front of us, it was Tasha's. Of all the people we had to run into today, it had to be her. Jream must've noticed my mood change because she asked me whether or not I was good. To answer her question, no. I was absolutely not good. I couldn't let my sister see me beat a bitch up on her first week in the city.

"Fuck it. C'mon we're good." I hit the buzzer for Lumps apartment and we walk right in. Four flights of stairs later we made it to Lumps door. *Why the hell was Tasha here? Was Lil Man okay?* I knocked a few times and got no answer so I knocked a few more times. Tasha opens the door in her panties and bra and at that moment I knew this had absolutely nothing to do with the baby.

"Hey, Toot-Toot. Come on in."
I rolled my eyes as hard as I could, grabbed Jreams hand and brushed right past Tasha and her stank ass PINK boy shorts.
"Where's Lump?" I asked.
"He's in our bedroom. Hold on, let me get him."

Our bedroom? Oh, this girl is on drugs. Why is Lump laid up with her anyway? That much couldn't have changed in a few weeks. I see Lump turning the corner from *his* bedroom with his boxers on, he's also shirtless and isn't wearing any socks.

"Hey, babygirl. Been a minute."
"You tweakin like a muthafucka, on God. Why is Tasha here?"
"It was just a lil hit, Tootie. Chill out." He looks over at Jream, "Who this is?"
"I'm Jream. You might wanna tell yo old lady to answer the door with some clothes next time."
"My old lady?, he chuckles, "Where you from, lord?"

"Nawlins."

"Jream, from New Orleans...", he looks back over at me and repeats it again. I can tell he was beginning to put two and two together.

"Yea, nigga. Damn."

"So this is her, huh? Man, you look just like TT and Tootie, on my son."

Jream smiles and responds, "Yea, I guess we got some strong genes."

"Mhm. Tootie, check it out." He motions for me to walk with him to the kitchen. I can tell where this conversation was headed.

"What, Lump?"

"Yo ass goin ku, you done brought yo whole ass sister back home."

"Before you start, my mama already knows. Don't go telling nobody else though."

"Well, what's she like?"

"You can find out for yourself if we go back and sit with her instead of standing here talkin' about her."

We walk back over to Jream and Tasha who was now sitting across from her, this time fully clothed. Why won't this girl just disappear and leave all of us alone? Good thing I have a big sister around now, we'll run this hoe down together if we have too. I almost forgot how fake Tasha was until I saw how friendly she was acting towards Jream. She went from Joi off of *Friday* to Claire

Huxtable in a matter of minutes. I can tell from the look on Jreams face that we had inherited the same low tolerance for bullshit the entire time Tasha was talking to her. I couldn't help but laugh.

"What's funny, Toot-Toot?"
"The fact that you think you share any room in this house with my cousin, that's what's funny, Sha-Sha." I gave her a fake ass smile and a wink just to get under her skin.
"William, get your cousin."
"*William, get your cousin.*" I mocked.
"Sis, you good?", Jream asked in a fairly intimidating yet calm tone. Enough to let Tasha and I both know she was ready for whatever.
"Yea, she don't wanna see me so I ain't worried about her at all."
"On my son, *we* ain't worried about her at all." Lump chimed in.

We started laughing and I motioned for Jream to get up so that we could leave. We would just have to catch up with *William* a little later because I was two seconds off of Tasha's ass and from the looks of it Jream wasn't too far behind. So, we left her there to play house for a day. Goofy ass.

"Nawlins."

"Jream, from New Orleans...", he looks back over at me and repeats it again. I can tell he was beginning to put two and two together.

"Yea, nigga. Damn."

"So this is her, huh? Man, you look just like TT and Tootie, on my son."

Jream smiles and responds, "Yea, I guess we got some strong genes."

"Mhm. Tootie, check it out." He motions for me to walk with him to the kitchen. I can tell where this conversation was headed.

"What, Lump?"

"Yo ass goin ku, you done brought yo whole ass sister back home."

"Before you start, my mama already knows. Don't go telling nobody else though."

"Well, what's she like?"

"You can find out for yourself if we go back and sit with her instead of standing here talkin' about her."

We walk back over to Jream and Tasha who was now sitting across from her, this time fully clothed. Why won't this girl just disappear and leave all of us alone? Good thing I have a big sister around now, we'll run this hoe down together if we have too. I almost forgot how fake Tasha was until I saw how friendly she was acting towards Jream. She went from Joi off of *Friday* to Claire

Huxtable in a matter of minutes. I can tell from the look on Jreams face that we had inherited the same low tolerance for bullshit the entire time Tasha was talking to her. I couldn't help but laugh.

"What's funny, Toot-Toot?"
"The fact that you think you share any room in this house with my cousin, that's what's funny, Sha-Sha." I gave her a fake ass smile and a wink just to get under her skin.
"William, get your cousin."
"*William, get your cousin.*" I mocked.
"Sis, you good?", Jream asked in a fairly intimidating yet calm tone. Enough to let Tasha and I both know she was ready for whatever.
"Yea, she don't wanna see me so I ain't worried about her at all."
"On my son, *we* ain't worried about her at all." Lump chimed in.

    We started laughing and I motioned for Jream to get up so that we could leave. We would just have to catch up with *William* a little later because I was two seconds off of Tasha's ass and from the looks of it Jream wasn't too far behind. So, we left her there to play house for a day. Goofy ass.

SIX.

Jream was only going to be in the city for one more day before she had to head back to school. Although it had only been a week spent with her, it felt like she'd been here forever. But, I had one more person that I wanted her to meet before she left and that was Twon. As my older sister it just made sense for her to feel out my new guy. So, I called Twon up to come to the house because I had someone I wanted him to meet.

"Someone you want me to meet? I know everybody that you know, Tiffany."
"You don't know her, though. She's family."
"Aight. Lemme go handle some things first and imma text you when I'm close."
"Okay."

I hung up the phone and started filling Jream in on what I could wrap my head around so far. Everything else I was going to leave up to her own interpretation.

"So what you gone do when he goes off to school? I don't wanna scare you but, college brings the hoe out of niggas."
"It's not like he's my *nigga*. He's got about a month left before he leaves so I'll worry about that when I have to."
"So y'all just messin' around? I'm not taking this nigga serious if that's the case."
"He's worth you meeting. I *need* you to meet him."

    Twon finally made it by the house and after giving him the run down on my long lost sister, he was just as speechless as I'd expected him to be. All he could say was, "wow", and kept looking back and forth at me and then Jream and then me again. Is it weird that a part of me was insecure? I know I've got it goin' on, don't get me wrong, but Jream was a *woman.* She was older, fuller in the hips and everywhere else, beautiful, and eccentric. If I were a dude she'd definitely be my type. What if Twon saw all of her and realized he no longer wanted any of me? I sound crazy, she hasn't even been here more than two weeks and I was already developing little sister syndrome.

"So you don't think any of this is crazy?", I asked Twon in hopes of breaking this awkward silence,
"Nah, I've seen crazier shit. Trust me. This actually kind of cool."
"Cool…", I said.

"Cool."

"I hope this ain't how y'all communicate on the regular. Cause if so, you need to get you a guy with a larger vocabulary."

    Twon and I look at each other and all three of us started laughing. This was somewhat the last piece to the puzzle and it felt good to have some other people to enjoy besides Lump. I'm even tempted to put a label on Twon and I's relationship status. He's adjusted to me so effortlessly and I definitely didn't expect to be falling for him so fast.

Damn, I'm glad I didn't take that Uber ride alone that night.

***

LOSSES.

"TOOTIE!"

I roll over and out of my bed.
Look at my phone, **4:05 A.M.**
I've got 4 missed calls
              (2) Lump 2:40 A.M.

Twon 2:55 A.M.
Conny 4:00 A.M.

"TOOTIE! Baby, wake up!"

I can hear my mama yelling all the way from the kitchen screaming as if she was being mauled by a pack of wolves. I had no idea what was going on but I was frozen with fear at the thought of what could possibly have happened at four in the morning, with multiple missed phone calls, and in this vile ass city of Chicago. I, literally, could not fucking move. The next thing I hear are my mother's footsteps running up the stairs towards my room.

"Gotdamnit, Girl. You don't hear me calling you?! We've got to go to the hospital *now… RIGHT NOW.*"
"Mama, what's goin' on? Is it Ma?"

She shakes her head, no.

"Is it you? Are you sick or something?"

She shakes her head, no, again.

"Is it Lump?"

She looked at me and placed her hand over her stomach. I don't know what she was feeling but it must've been contagious because I immediately felt my stomach tighten and my breath shortening. Lump must've "handled" what he needed to handle and something didn't go as planned. I felt myself about to faint but before I could hit the floor my phone started ringing, it was Twon.

"Hello?"
"Baby girl, get to the hospital ASAP. I was almost there, man! He should've called me earlier! FUCK!"
"Twon, what happened? Calm down and just tell me what happened to Lump."
"They fuckin shot my nigga up, lord. A bunch of hoe ass niggas set him up. He went to settle that shit with Tay but he was supposed to hit me the moment things started lookin' sketchy. What was supposed to be just him and Tay, ended up being him, Tay and six other niggas!"

I could feel the tears rolling down my face like hot lava. I hung up the phone before Twon could even finish telling me anything and immediately rushed me and my mama out of the house. That ten minute car ride felt like ten years before we'd finally made it to the ICU. Auntie Lonnie and Ma were already there. Auntie Shay was in the corner in a heated argument with one of the nurses and Uncle Will was doing his best to keep her from hauling off and slapping the spit out of this lady's mouth.

"Ma, what's Auntie Shay yelling about?"
"They won't let us see him yet. Son of a bitches keep telling us we need to wait for the doctor."
"He could be dead by then!", I yelled.

   I rush over to Auntie Shay and try explaining to the nurse how necessary it is that at least one of us is able to see Lump even of the rest of us have to stay put. Eventually she gave in and allowed the "mother to be the only one to see the patient." Watching Auntie Lonnie walk onto the other side of those doors felt like hell. We couldn't do anything in that moment but wait. Everything seemed unreal. I was just with this nigga a few weeks ago, laughing and kickin' it and here we are awaiting the news of whether he's dead or alive. I looked at my phone at the last time he'd called me, I guess I was in such shock earlier that I hadn't realized he left a voicemail. I hit play:

Saturday 2:41 A.M. 0:28
"Hey babygirl, I didn't expect you to answer so you good. Just letting you know I'm handling this shit from that lil situation a while back. I know yo nosey ass wanted to know what was up so I'm just tellin you. I fuck

around and be chillin back at the slot by the time you wake up and even hear this shit. But aight, lord. I love you."

What the fuck, Lump?

About thirty-five minutes had gone by of us just waiting and praying. Finally, we saw a tall black man in blue scrubs come walking our way. He didn't have anything in his hands nor did he have anyone with him, it was Lumps doctor. I felt it, the bad news, the lump in my throat, the burning sensation behind my eyes.

"Are you all the Jenkins family?"
"Yes." I answered.
"I'm Doctor Jeff Garrison. I just stepped out of surgery. William, was shot ten times. Once in his shoulder, three times in his back, twice in his left leg, once in his neck, his hand and his stomach. We prepared him for surgery immediately…"
"But?" I asked, knowing that there was bad news.
"*But*, unfortunately one of the bullets in his back pierced his lung causing it to collapse. It had already done more than enough damage before he even made it to the hospital. I'm sorry."

And just like that, one of the best loves I've ever known was taken from me. My best friend in the entire world doesn't even exist anymore. I was furious, sick, confused, enraged, and sad as hell all at the same time. Usually, any other time where I felt this terrible I'd call Lump and he'd come grab me and take me to get some ice cream or something. But, who the fuck do I call now?

What the *fuck*, Lump?

SEVEN.

    I've been sitting in my room with the lights off and the curtains closed for the past six days. I haven't gotten up to do anything more than pee and I've probably had about as much to eat as a pigeon in a park. My phone has been on "Do Not Disturb" since we left the hospital the night Lump died. I don't want to talk to anyone because there's nothing they can possibly say to help this feel any less real. The funeral is in two days and I can't even tell you where or what time the service is, I've been doing my absolute best not to include myself in any of the arrangements. Burying my cousin? Burying my best friend, confidant, my *brother*. I didn't have anything left in me besides vengeance. Tay and them niggas were gonna get what the fuck was coming for them and this time *I* was going to handle it. I won't be doing the trigger pulling but I was definitely going to be calling the shots. All I needed was a plan good enough to get me in and out without having to plan another funeral. There's no way in hell I was just going to let this be. Lump would go to war for me... Lump would settle the score.

Along with the fact that I hadn't been outside of the house, no one had been here to see either me or mama. That was until today, at least, because I'd heard the front door alarm go off for the first time this week. I could faintly hear a man's voice in conversation with my mom but I couldn't make out who it was. The next thing I heard was footsteps moving closer towards my bedroom door. It had been shut closed for days so it was necessary to knock. I heard my mom saying my name a few times but I, physically, couldn't respond.

"Tiffany. Tiffany, you've got someone here to see you, baby, can we come in?"

I just laid there looking at the door, not saying a word. Once the door opened I realized the voice that I'd heard was Twon's, he was standing behind mama with a bouquet of sunflowers and what looked to be a bag of food. I can't deny that I was happy to see him, I just didn't have the strength to show it.

"Hey, babygirl, I brought you some stuff. I know you not eatin'." I didn't move. I didn't say anything. I just looked at him and before I knew it, I was crying. "Come here,

Tiffany. I got you." I rolled into his lap and he rubbed my back until I was composed enough to say anything.

"You gotta kill him."
"Huh? Baby what you talkin' bout? Kill who?"
"You gotta kill Tay for killing Lump, period."
"Aye, chill out. You don't need to worry about anything like that, you just need to focus on gettin' yoself together."

I raised up and looked him square in his eyes.

"Fuck it, then. Just let Lump be another nigga that lost his life to some lame ass shit."
"Tiffany, you know this ain't you. Besides, the last thing Lump would want is for you to be doin' some goofy shit."
"Well, what you gone do, nigga? You're his best friend ain't you?"
"First of all, mind yo tongue. I'm not the one you need to be checkin', imma handle it."

    I rolled my eyes and grabbed the bag of food, just because I wasn't eating didn't mean I wasn't hungry as hell. This conversation wasn't doing anything but making me anxious so I was pretty much done talking Besides, if he wasn't going to do anything about it I was going to take matters into my own hands.

"Thanks for the food and the flowers. How'd you know to get sunflowers?"

"I remember Lump getting you one every year for your birthday. He said you were really into them so... no problem."

"You pay attention." I said while smiling.

"Yea. I've been paying attention for years. I know all your favorites. I know you hate the smell of cinnamon, but I've watched you tear a Cinnabon up in three bites. I know you love going to the movies the day it premieres because you feel like you're apart of the conversation. I know you enjoy going to the bookstore and the library as a pass time. I notice how you swing your right arm when you walk and put all your weight on your left leg when you skate. I notice you only wear your hair parted on the left side of your face to hide that cut Lump gave you when we were little. I noticed the day you were finally starting to feel me and you thought I wasn't paying any attention to the fact that you were staring at me the entire time."

"Boy, bye. Wasn't nobody even lookin' at you."

He looked at me with this grin on his face.

"What?", I asked.
"You wanna know what else I noticed?"

I stuff one last spoon full of broccoli and cheese soup in my mouth before answering.

"I noticed that there's a chance you may love me, but you haven't figured out how to let yourself say it."
"How you figure that?"
"Because there's also a chance I may love you too, and the only way that's possible is if I felt it was mutual."

He was right, I did love him. He was everything I could have hoped for in a guy. On top of that, he was the only nigga Lump ever approved of for me and that meant more to me than anything.

"So say it, then."
"Say what?" he asked.
"Say what you feel."
"No matter what happens or who you end up with, I'll always love you. If you need anything from me I'll always be there for you. Whatever I can give, is yours. It doesn't matter who I'm with, I got you. That's a fact."

I looked that beautiful ass man dead in his eyes and without even checking with my brain first, I said what my heart needed to say, "I love you, too."

***

I've been so many places in my life and time
I've song a lot of songs
I've made some bad rhymes

*I've acted out my life on stages, with ten thousand people watchin
But we're alone now, and I'm singing this song to you…*

It wasn't Jill, but it was close enough.

 Seeing Twon the other night pushed me to get up and "get myself together", as he so eloquently put it. I woke up to Donny Hathaway's *A Song For You* playing from the kitchen. When I was nine, my daddy decided to throw me a themed birthday party. That year it was "Tiffany's Talents: A Showcase", where all the kids would pick a talent and perform it for me as a gift. I remember Lump getting on that stage and everyone expecting him to rap or sing some Chris Brown song, but to everyone's surprise he started singing Donny Hathaway. I don't know where he'd learned it from but he sounded so good! I was glad mama decided to play it this morning.

"Goodmorning."
"Goodmorning, Tootie. How you feelin?"
"Like I'm about to bury my best friend in a few hours," I said before stuffing a piece of a pancake in my mouth.
"I understand. This shit is crazy. I hate it here sometimes, I swear I do. We are both definitely due for a vacation very soon."
"How soon?" I asked.

"Why? You got something coming up?"

I didn't want to head off too soon before knowing what Twon was going to do about Tay. He may have thought I was talking out my ass the other night, but a large part of me was one-hundred percent serious. I can't leave the country just yet.

"Nah, not really. I just wanted to make sure I had enough time to prepare and everything."
"Is two weeks enough time for ya?"
"Yea… yea that's cool."

We walked into the church in a single filed line just like in elementary school. Auntie Lonnie and Uncle Will were first alongside their other two kids, TJ and Cyrus. Tasha was right behind them with Lil Man in her arms, crying her entire life away. Then Ma and the rest of her kids, then me and the other cousins followed. I couldn't look out into the pews because it all seemed too real and I definitely couldn't look towards the casket because it doesn't get any realer than that. We took up the first two pews with front row tickets to the second worst day of my life, losing my daddy was the first. I didn't care to smile at anyone, I didn't care to hear them give their condolences, I didn't even care to speak. Relatives I hadn't seen since Lump and I were babies crowded around me and the family like jehovah's witnesses, I couldn't take it anymore.

     I was suffocating on that pew so I got up to get some fresh air. On my way out the door I spotted someone standing on the steps. She's got on a long black dress and a scarf tied on her head like Erykah Badu. I can barely make out the side of her face but I immediately recognized the sunflower tattoo on her neck.

"Jream?"
She turns around with this big smile on her face, "Hey, lil sis."
I ran into her arms and bury my face into her chest. I didn't cry or scream. I just needed to breath and for some reason the air I needed was tucked away in Jream's bosom.
"When did you get here? How'd you even know what was goin on?"
"Conny called me the day after it happened and told me to come up and check on you. She said you weren't really talkin to anyone else and to see if I could give it a try. I'm sorry, luv."
"Yea, me too. I'm glad you're here. Lump was my go-to for as long as I can remember. Twon's been amazing and Conny's always been my girl. I don't know.. I just need someone else."
"I got you. The semesters over with so I'll be able to stay for as long as you need me to."
"Good, cause imma need your help with somethin'."

EIGHT.

I keep replaying Lumps voicemail over and over again. I wonder if I had answered would it have made a difference in outcomes. Lump didn't listen to too many people but he always listened to me, he cared about my opinion. Had I picked up the phone I could've talked him out of meeting up with Tay that night. He would've been here with me and not six feet in the ground. I know how Twon must feel knowing that he couldn't even pull through as they'd planned. I noticed I'd spent so much time wallowing in my own pain that I hadn't thought to ask anyone else about there's. So, I called Twon. We hadn't talked since the funeral.

"Hey, Twon."
"Hey, baby girl."
"U good?"
"Yea, I'm always good. Wbu?"

"I'm as good as I'm gonna be. I was just checking to see how you were handling things. I never got the chance to ask."
"I mean, shit. To be honest with you I feel guilty as hell. Had I been there wouldn't none of that shit happened like it did."
"True. It's not your fault, g. It ain't none of our faults. I appreciate you being such a good friend to him."

It was quiet for a minute on both of our ends. I don't know why, but for some reason I felt uneasy. I hadn't had time to sit and honestly think about the sequence of events leading up to Lump being shot. I guess I never had the time to between crying and being depressed for the past month. But, oddly enough, in this very moment I'm every bit of curious.

"Babe, what happened that night with Lump?"
"What you mean?"
"I mean how'd he end up goin to Tay's alone?"
"I was supposed to ride down there with him but… something came up and I said I'd just meet him there. It was a quick run so I was positive I was gone get to him in time."
"How'd you find out once everything went down?"
"You remember Taco?"
"Yea. What he got to do with anything?"
"You know he stay across the street from Tay, or whatever. He said he heard some shooting so he peep the scene and say he seen Lump laid out. As soon as I got the call, I called you. To be honest, baby, all that shit happened so fast I'm probably messing the whole story up. You don't even need to be

worried about none of this. You gone get yourself worked up again."

"You right. Let me hyu later though."

"Aight, baby. I love you."

After that conversation, I immediately started dialing Jreams number. I had to talk to someone who knew absolutely no one from around here because, clearly, I couldn't trust anybody. Twon was lying and it was obvious. Taco and his grandmother moved out of K-Town three months ago due to some other crazy shit Tay had started on their block. So, how'd *he* end up being the one to make the call about Lump getting shot? I needed to talk this confusion out with someone and that someone *had* to be Jream.

***

"Wait wait, hold on. Tootie, you're talkin' too damn fast. Twon set who up?"

"Lump!"

"And you know this, because...?"

"Because I ain't a goofy."

"So what's next?"

"I don't have any *real* evidence so I gotta do some more research. I'm gonna need your help for a couple of days, you're the only one I trust at the moment."

"Cool. Come to the hotel and we can come up with something."

"Getting my Lyft now."

      I made it to Jreams hotel in twenty-two minutes, I made my way up to her room and knocked three times. I could hear some rustling around and eventually the door swung open. Jream was standing there in a towel hanging half-way off of her body and a face mask that looked to have been freshly applied.

      "Girl, are you having a spa treatment while I'm having a mental breakdown?", I ask with my arms folded and my mother's best neck roll. She rolls her eyes and motions for me to walk in, it smelled like vanilla. Her stuff was all over the place and she obviously had a lot of time to herself cooped up in this suite. It amazes me how a college budget allows a three hundred dollar per night stay but that's neither here nor there. We've got way more important things to clear up.

"So have you come up with anything new?," she asked as she wipes the green avocado mask off of her face. I shake my head "no" and focus my attention towards the view from her room. I had nothing. Nothing more than I'd already known, at least. But, how was I going to prove that my boyfriend set my cousin up to get killed? I hadn't come to this revelation until just now! I tried my best to think back and retrace steps and everything but my mind was too cloudy. Then suddenly I remembered that night Twon came over to my house.

"The phone call!", I yelled.
"Girl, what the hell?! I nearly jumped out of my skin!"
"Jream, there was a phone call Twon made the night he came over to my house. I thought he was on the phone talkin to some girl but he said it was 'business' and that I shouldn't worry about it. What if that was *the* phone call that set Lump up to get shot?"
"Only way you gone find that out is if you knew who he was on the phone with. You got the code to his phone?"
"No, but I can get it."
"Call his ass up and tell him we wanna kick it. Find a way to get ahold of his phone and search his call history back as far as you can get it. Boom. Case solved."

    By the time I took my focus away from the window Jream was already dressed and ready to go. I hadn't stopped to appreciate the fact that I have an older sister until now. Lump had always had my back no matter what the case was and here comes Jream, filling the void. I texted Twon and told him to meet us downtown in front of the tower so we could show Jream around. Before Jream and I met up with him we went over how I'd get ahold of the phone without seeming suspicious.

"Just ask him if you can use it for a second."
I looked at her in annoyance, "Jream, what nigga you know just gives his phone up without a good reason?"
"Good point."
She then reaches for my phone, I hand it over and she turns it off.
"Act like you left your phone in the Lyft & you need his to call it. I'll just say mine is dead or something."

She tosses my phone in her purse and we waited about five minutes until we saw Twon walking towards us and to our surprise he wasn't alone.

"Hey, baby. Wassup, Jream."
"Hey", I say while waiting for him to introduce his uninvited sidekick.
"Oh, my bad, this is LJ. He used to kick it with me and Lump back in the day. I thought I'd bring him along so Jream wouldn't have to play third wheel, you feel me?"
"Nigga, I ain't ask for no date", Jream snapped.
"Yea, bae. We just wanted to kick it, that's all. She would've been fine."
"Well, damn, he's here now. Fuck we gone do about it? Cmon."

Jream and I looked at each other knowing we would have to rethink our plan now that we had an extra pair of eyes glued to our every move. Who is this nigga, anyway? LJ? Lump never mentioned an LJ to me and I knew all of Lumps friends, new and old. He definitely wouldn't be hanging around this nigga, he had trouble written all over him. The man was wearing black ones. There was no doubt in my mind that he robbed and killed. Lump wasn't squeaky clean but he was extremely mindful of who he let around him and even more mindful of who he let around me. I've never seen this muthafucka in my life.

"So, you knew my cousin?" I asked LJ.
"Yea. I knew him from back when we were shorties."
"Did you come to the funeral?"
"Nah. I couldn't make it, but I'm sorry for your loss."
"Why am I just now seeing you? Everybody knows Lump and I did everything together and he never mentioned you to me."
"Yea. We fell out for a few years over some hoe who was tryna play both of us like some goofies. I guess she laid it thick on Lump cause he chose her over our friendship. But, it is what it is. No love lost."

I don't know what was getting under my skin the most. The fact that Twon ambushed us with this random ass dude or the fact that this random ass dude was no friend of Lump's. Part of me really wanted to know why Twon was so comfortable with bringing him around after Lump was dead and gone. It was clear to me that even though Lump cut off all communication with LJ, *he* hadn't done the same. Another red flag.

I started to text Jream on the low but I remembered she had my phone stowed away in her purse. I was tired of stalling so this was the perfect time to initiate the plan.

"Aye, Jream, call my phone right quick", I asked while dramatically patting down my pockets.
"Damn. My phones dead, sis. Where'd you last have it?
"I think I left it in the lyft. Bae, let me use your phone to call it right quick."

I put my hand out hoping no one noticed the slight tremble I had. To my surprise he offered it up with no hesitation. I immediately call my phone so that everything seemed believable, but of course it went to voicemail each time. I glanced over at Jream hinting for her to create some sort of distraction so that neither Twon nor LJ could focus too much on what I was doing. She caught on quickly and instantly sparked up a conversation with the two of them, asking about random buildings and shit. This gave me at least a couple of minutes to scan the call log. Clearly, Twon doesn't make too many phone calls because I didn't have to search too far down to find the day and time I was looking for.

3125556123

I memorized it as quickly as I could but my finger must've trembled a little too hard and I accidentally pressed the number. I couldn't end the call quick enough before I heard ringing from another phone close by. The moment I saw LJ reach into his back pocket I felt my stomach hit the pavement. It was him! It was LJ!

NINE.

At that moment, Jream and I were standing flat footed and stuck by what we had just discovered. As hard as it was not to windmill this nigga, I had to keep up the act and calmly hand Twon his phone back. However, there was no way I could keep playing it cool and hang out with either of these dudes for the next couple of hours. So, I made up some story about my mom needing me and Jream back at the crib. Twon offered us a ride but I immediately declined and Jream and I ended up taking the closest Lyft back to her hotel. Both of us were at a loss for words. I was sick to my stomach knowing that I had been *that* close to the people responsible for Lump no longer being alive. And to think I actually told that man I *loved* him. I mean, he had the audacity to bring his partner in crime around me and my sister? To have the one dude who I'd finally decided to give a chance screw me over like this is honestly the worst feeling. Once we made it back to Jreams room I dropped to the floor and cried uncontrollably.

"This isn't really happening", I sobbed. "This shit cannot be my reality."

Jream walked me over to the bed and I tucked myself away in her bosom. I didn't expect her to have too much to say being as though she and Lump had only met a couple of months ago. But, despite her not knowing what to say, she always knew what to do to comfort me in any moment.

"Oh, baby sis. It's sad, but it's life. You're gonna have moments where only the ones you love most can teach you the hardest lessons."

I thought to myself, "Well, what lesson is this?" Is it to stop trusting niggas all together? Is it to stop being so naive? What lesson did I have to learn by way of my cousin dying and my boyfriend being the culprit?

It doesn't make sense.

****

Since Lump's death I've been trying my hardest to understand the sequence of events from the moment he was shot until now. At times I even began questioning my role in everything. Did I let a nigga charm me so well that I couldn't see him plotting against my own flesh and blood? I mean, usually nothing gets past me. I'm an analyzer, an observer, a detailer, I pay attention to everything. So, how'd I miss this?! I tracked down my sister from a photo and a drunken conversation. *So, how did you miss this, Tiffany?* I've never had reason to be vengeful until now. I've never had reason to be skeptical until now. I've never had reason to target anyone until now. I lost something huge when my father died, but I lost everything in Lump's passing: my best friend, my cousin, my confidant, my bodyguard, my brother. And now those responsible for his death are about to lose everything they cherish as well.

Letter From The Author

For starters, *thank you* for coming this far with me. I appreciate all of the support thus far and I hope that everything I create is resonating with you in some way, shape or form. Secondly, how'd you like it? I left you hanging there for a reason. This story is not only my first fiction novel, but it is also part one of my first fiction *series*. So, don't worry, you'll see what sort of shit Tiffany gets herself into and where her sister ends up and how she tries to even the score and so on. It's going to be a page turner, I'm sure of it. It only gets better from here.

I actually have some more really good news. If you are a loyal reader then you are already familiar with my first book, *Brown Girl Proverb*, and so many people have been asking me for a part two. So, yea. You're gonna get it! That makes *two* series under my belt thanks to the support of my readers! Again, I appreciate you hanging around for as long as you have and I can assure you you're going to want to stick around even longer. Be sure to keep up with me and all that I have going on by visiting my website, www.browngirlproverb.com

But, for now here's a sneak peak at part two of Losses And Gains, the series…

I Love You
Favor, Peace & Blessings

Mimi

PART TWO.

ONE.

    Unlike most mornings, I woke up to mama listening to gospel music so I couldn't tell whether she was in a good mood or a bad one. Ma was more of the churchy type than the rest of us and my mama hardly ever played gospel music. It wasn't like she wasn't spiritual, she just wasn't religious. We didn't go to church every Sunday but she'd always remind me to pray and thank God. We only knew a few scriptures from the Bible but my mama used them at all the right moments. It just worked for us. So for her to start the morning off with gospel was pretty odd.

"Mama, you okay?", I ask before grabbing the plate she'd just stacked with pancakes.
"I don't know, Tootie."
"What you mean you don't know? Wassup?"
"I think these new clients are trying to play me. We were supposed to discuss percentages last night and no one got back to me. I've called four or five times and haven't gotten an answer or a call back. I would hate to have to turn up on these muthafuckas."
"Yea tell me about it," I whisper under my breath.

She turns the stove off and looks to me with her hand on her hip, "What's going on, Tootie?" I waited a few seconds contemplating whether or not I should reveal what Jream and I had uncovered yesterday or keep mama out of it. But, as I thought a little longer, she may actually be of some help.

"I know who's responsible for Lumps death."
"What the hell? Who?!"
"Twon. Twon and some dude named LJ."
"Twon? I know you lyin'. Who is LJ? Why would he want to hurt Lump?"
"Apparently all three of them used to be friends when they were younger but LJ and Lump fell out over a girl. I'm not sure how well that story plays out but that's all I know as of now."

She turned away from me for a few seconds in deep thought.

"What?", I asked.
"You said LJ? As in London James? He used to be Lumps neighbor when they were kids but I don't remember them being as close as he claims."
"So you know him?"
"Aw yea. I know that lil nigga, alright. In fact, his older brother Fatz and I made an arrangement about 8 months ago. If I'm not mistaken, that was around the time LJ got locked up for drug possession. With the money I helped his brother save he was able to get bonded out. Son of a bitch kills my nephew not even six months later."
"So what should we do? Go to the police?"
"And say what, Tiffany? They not gone help us any more than they claim they already have. I got this one."

Remember how I said there was more to my mother than just looks and money? This was it. Her whole demeanor changed and I could tell shit was about to take a turn for the worse. I texted Jream and told her to head this way as soon as she could. We needed all hands on deck.

Made in the
USA
Columbia, SC